W9-AAW-440

Language consultant: Betty Root

This is a Parragon Publishing book
This edition published in 2006

Parragon Publishing
Queen Street House
4 Queen Street
Bath BA1 1HE, UK

Copyright © Parragon Books Ltd 2003
All rights reserved. No part of this publication may be
reproduced, stored in a retrieval system or transmitted by any
means, electronic, mechanical, photocopying, recording or
otherwise without the prior permission of the copyright holder.

ISBN 1-84250-575-0
Printed in Malaysia

My Grandma is Great

Written by Gaby Goldsack
Illustrated by Sara Walker

p

My grandma is **great.**
She's gentle, kind, and lots of fun.

Sometimes when Mom and Dad go out for the evening, I go to stay at Grandma's house.

I always have a **fantastic** time, because my grandma makes me feel special.

Sometimes she gets carried away!

Grandma never gets angry ...
even when I make a terrible mess.

And she always likes my cooking.
I can't wait for her to taste my muffins.

Grandma always knows exactly what I like.
She gives me the **yummiest** food.

But that's our little secret—
don't tell Mom and Dad!

My grandma likes me to help around the house. She calls me her "little helper."

Grandma doesn't care how much noise
I make. She even bought me this terrific
set of drums.

Mom and Dad will be really pleased!

BASH!

BANG!

BASH!

My grandma has lots of interesting hobbies.

She's the **coolest** grandma I know.

And she knits me **fabulous** sweaters.

Well...my giraffe likes them anyway.

My grandma loves playing games.
"Catch, Grandma!"

Grandma's favorite game is hide-and-seek.
I usually hide while she looks for me.
I'm so good at hiding that she never finds me.

Grandma gives the **best** hugs ever!

And she lets me stay up late.

At bedtime, Grandma tells me funny stories about Dad when he was a little boy. She says that he was quite naughty.

She makes me laugh so much that I get hiccups. My grandma's so great that she knows how to get rid of them.

I'm always sad when I kiss Grandma goodbye.
But she only lives next door, so I go over to
see her when I want, because...

... my grandma is GREAT!